A Note to Parents and Caregivers:

Read-it! Readers are for children who are just starting on the amazing road to reading. These beautiful books support both the acquisition of reading skills and the love of books.

The PURPLE LEVEL presents basic topics and objects using high frequency words and simple language patterns.

The RED LEVEL presents familiar topics using common words and repeating sentence patterns.

The BLUE LEVEL presents new ideas using a larger vocabulary and varied sentence structure.

The YELLOW LEVEL presents more challenging ideas, a broad vocabulary, and wide variety in sentence structure.

The GREEN LEVEL presents more complex ideas, an extended vocabulary range, and expanded language structures.

The ORANGE LEVEL presents a wide range of ideas and concepts using challenging vocabulary and complex language structures.

When sharing a book with your child, read in short stretches, pausing often to talk about the pictures. Have your child turn the pages and point to the pictures and familiar words. And be sure to reread favorite stories or parts of stories.

There is no right or wrong way to share books with children. Find time to read with your child, and pass on the legacy of literacy.

Adria F. Klein, Ph.D.
Professor Emeritus
California State University
San Bernardino, California

Editor: Shelly Lyons
Designer: Tracy Davies
Page Production: Melissa Kes
Art Director: Nathan Gassman
Associate Managing Editor: Christianne Jones
The illustrations in this book were created with colored pencil.

Picture Window Books
151 Good Counsel Drive
P.O. Box 669
Mankato, MN 56002-0669
877-845-8392
www.picturewindowbooks.com

Printed in the United States of America.

Library of Congress Cataloging-in-Publication Data
O'Hearn, Michael, 1972-
How Spirit Dog made the Milky Way : a retelling of a Cherokee legend /
retold by Michael O'Hearn ; illustrated by Roberta Collier-Morales.
p. cm. — (Read-it! readers : legends)
ISBN 978-1-4048-4846-7 (library binding)
1. Cherokee Indians—Folklore. 2. Milky Way—Folklore.
I. Collier-Morales, Roberta. II. Title.
E99.C5O44 2009
398.2089'97557—dc22   2008006329

How Spirit Dog Made the Milky Way

A Retelling of a Cherokee Legend

retold by Michael O'Hearn
illustrated by Roberta Collier-Morales

Special thanks to our reading adviser:

Adria F. Klein, Ph.D.
Professor Emeritus, California State University
San Bernardino, California

PICTURE WINDOW BOOKS
Minneapolis, Minnesota

There is a river of stars called the Milky Way.
This is how it came to be.

Many seasons ago, an old man and woman lived at the edge of a Cherokee village. Their home stood beneath a thick oak tree. The oak tree gave them shade from the sun.

A stream flowed nearby. There, the couple could fish and soak their feet.

They enjoyed the quiet.

The old man spent most days fishing. The old woman worked in the garden. She grew corn, pumpkins, potatoes, and beans.

The old woman picked corn. Then she ground it to make cornmeal. She left the cornmeal outside at night. It was for the next day's bread.

Each day, the old woman made bread.

Each afternoon, she sat with her husband by the stream. They munched the bread and a bit of pumpkin. Each night, they sat and watched the stars.

One morning, the old woman discovered her cornmeal was missing. The bucket was tipped over. It was covered in scratches.

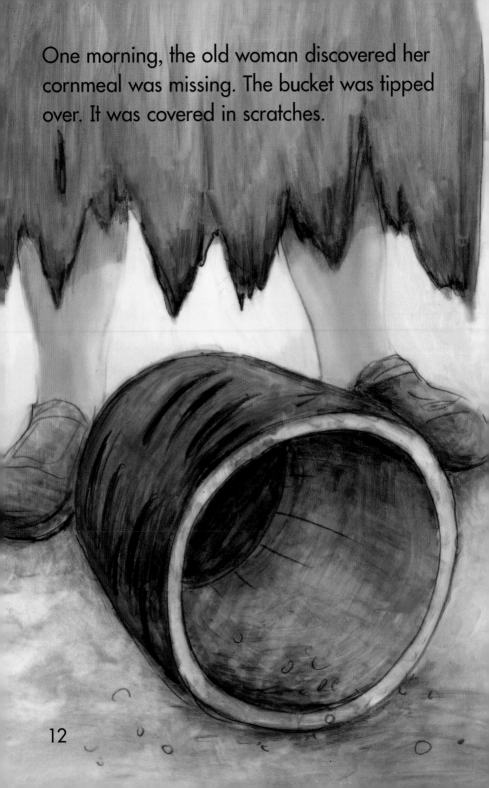

"Our cornmeal has been stolen!" the old woman told her husband.

13

Nearby, the couple found golden bits of cornmeal scattered across the dirt. The cornmeal looked like stars in the night sky.

They also found the paw prints of a giant dog.

The old couple went about their daily work.
They ate a dinner of fish and beans.

That night, they huddled under their covers. They were afraid the dog would return. But they heard only the chirping of crickets. The old man and woman soon fell asleep.

17

The next morning, the couple stepped outside. Again, they found the cornmeal bucket empty.

And again, they found dog tracks.

The old man and woman called their neighbors
to a meeting. They told them what had
happened. They showed everyone the huge
paw prints.

"It is the great spirit dog!" someone shouted.

Everyone agreed. There was much nodding and mumbling. The couple asked how they could get rid of the troublesome dog. No one could answer.

Finally, the old woman said that everyone should come back that night. She told her neighbors to bring noisemakers and drums.

"We will frighten away the sneaky dog!"
she said.

23

All afternoon, the old couple went about their work. They made more cornmeal than usual. They hoped to lure the dog back.

That night, the neighbors arrived. They carried rattles, drums, buckets, stones, and sticks. They hid in the old couple's house. They kept very quiet. The world was quiet. Even the crickets did not peep.

Finally, everyone heard the dog outside. It pawed at the bucket. It munched the cornmeal.

"Now!" the old woman shouted.

The neighbors shook their rattles and beat their drums. They banged on buckets with stones and sticks. They hollered and wailed. The racket was enough to frighten even a spirit dog.

The giant dog bounded into the air. Moonlight shone on its silvery coat. Cornmeal fell from its mouth.

The cornmeal clung to the sky behind the dog and left a trail where the animal had fled. It formed a thick band of golden flecks. The flecks looked like a river of stars.

The spirit dog never returned.

Some nights, the old couple sat with their toes in the stream. They stared at the dog's trail hanging in the sky. They remembered how their neighbors helped scare the dog away.

More *Read-it!* Readers

Bright pictures and fun stories help you practice your reading skills. Look for more books at your level.

How Spirit Dog Made the Milky Way:
A Retelling of a Cherokee Legend
King Arthur and the Black Knight
King Arthur and the Sword in the Stone
Mato the Bear and Devil's Tower:
A Retelling of a Lakota Legend
Robin Hood and the Golden Arrow
Robin Hood and the Tricky Butcher

On the Web

FactHound offers a safe, fun way to find Web sites related to topics in this book. All of the sites on FactHound have been researched by our staff.

1. Visit *www.facthound.com*

2. Type in this special code:
   1404848460

3. Click on the FETCH IT button.

Your trusty FactHound will fetch the best sites for you!
A complete list of *Read-it!* Readers is available on our Web site:
www.picturewindowbooks.com

32